D1108525

To my dearest parents, who read so
many stories to us all. —M.D.

Published by Greenleaf Book Group Press
Austin, Texas
www.gbgpress.com

Distributed by Greenleaf Book Group LLC

For ordering information or special discounts for bulk purchases, please contact
Greenleaf Book Group LLC at PO Box 91869, Austin, TX 78709, 512.891.6100.

Design and composition by Greenleaf Book Group LLC
Cover design by Greenleaf Book Group LLC
Illustrations by Phil Wilson

Publisher's Cataloging-In-Publication Data (Prepared by The Donohue Group, Inc.)

DeLand, M. Maitland.
Baby Santa's worldwide Christmas adventure / M. Maitland DeLand ; illustrations by Phil Wilson. -- 1st ed.

p. : col. ill. ; cm. -- ([Baby Santa series ; v. 2])

ISBN: 978-1-60832-062-2

1. Santa Claus--Juvenile fiction. 2. Christmas--Juvenile fiction. 3. Travel--
Juvenile fiction. 4. Santa Claus--Fiction. 5. Christmas--Fiction. 6. Travel--Fiction. I.
Wilson, Phil, 1948- II. Title. III. Title: Worldwide Christmas adventure

PZ7.D37314 Bb 2010

[E]   2010927571

Part of the Tree Neutral™ program, which offsets the number of trees consumed in
the production and printing of this book by taking proactive steps, such as planting
trees in direct proportion to the number of trees used: www.treeneutral.com.

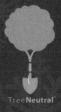

Manufactured by Imago on acid-free paper
Manufactured in China, June 2010
Batch No. 1

10 11 12 13 14   10 9 8 7 6 5 4 3 2 1

First Edition

Baby Santa's

WORLDWIDE CHRISTMAS ADVENTURE

M. Maitland DeLand, M.D.

WITH ILLUSTRATIONS BY PHIL WILSON

GREENLEAF
BOOK GROUP PRESS

On a blustery Christmas Eve at the North Pole, Santa walked from his workshop to the barn where he kept his sleigh. He wanted to make sure the sleigh was in tip-top condition for the night's important journey.

He opened the barn door, stepped inside, and found—nothing! The sleigh was gone!

Santa ran from the empty barn, dashed to the workshop, and burst through the door.

"What's wrong, Santa?" Head Elf Stanley asked.

"My sleigh is not in the barn," Santa panted. "Where is it?"

"Oh my goodness," Head Elf Stanley gasped. "The elves in maintenance took the sleigh for repairs last week. They said they would return it this morning. I'll find out where it is, Santa."

"I've got bad news," Elf Isabelle told Head Elf Stanley. "When we were pulling the sleigh out of the shop, one of the runners broke. We're trying to fix it, but I'm afraid it won't be ready in time!"

Head Elf Stanley broke the news to Santa.

"But today is Christmas Eve. I have to deliver all of the presents *tonight*. What am I going to do?"

"Maybe I can help," said someone in a high voice.

Baby Santa jumped up from his small work table—made just for him by the elves. He was choosing the right gifts for the remaining children on Santa's Christmas list.

"I'm sure we can think of something," he said.

"But, Baby Santa, there is no substitute for my sleigh. It can go anywhere in the world."

"It can sail over mountains and oceans."

"And can squeeze between tall buildings."

"It's a magical sleigh," Santa sighed. "I just don't see how we can replace it in time."

"Hmmm," Baby Santa said. "People all around the world travel in different ways. Can't we use their cars, planes, boats, and bicycles? You're magic, too, Santa. You can make it work."

"You're right," Santa said, a smile spreading across his face. "We just have to be creative."

Head Elf Stanley got the elves started on a plan.

Soon, Baby Santa and the elves had mapped a route for Santa all over the world.

"There's only one problem," Santa pointed out. "If I'm not riding in the sleigh, I will have to carry all the gifts. Someone will have to travel with me to guide my way."

"I'll do it!" Baby Santa squeaked.

"Ho, ho, ho," Santa laughed. "That's a great idea, son."

"Don't forget your earmuffs, Baby Santa," Mrs. Claus said.

"Thanks, Momma," Baby Santa called as he and Santa climbed into their reindeer taxi.

B aby Santa guided his poppa
through England . . .

France . . .

23

Italy . . .

Australia . . .

Japan...

$\mathcal{H}$awaii . . .

Argentina . . .

28

Egypt . . .

Canada . . .

Just as the sun rose in each town, boys and girls awoke to find presents waiting for them.

It took them a little longer than usual, but Santa and Baby Santa finally finished delivering all the presents and returned to the North Pole.

As Santa and Mrs. Claus tucked Baby Santa into bed, he stretched his arms out and yawned. He was exhausted.

"Get some rest, Baby Santa," Mrs. Claus said. "You worked hard tonight."

"Thank you, son," Santa added. "Christmas and all the children everywhere from near and far really needed your help. I'm so proud of you."

"It was fun, Poppa," Baby Santa smiled. He looked up at his Dad and said, "You know...

"The whole wide world really loves Christmas."